Ann H. Titus

Lunatic asylums - their use and abuse

A true narrative

Ann H. Titus

Lunatic asylums - their use and abuse
A true narrative

ISBN/EAN: 9783742833730

Manufactured in Europe, USA, Canada, Australia, Japa

Cover: Foto ©Andreas Hilbeck / pixelio.de

Ann H. Titus

Lunatic asylums - their use and abuse

LUNATIC ASYLUMS.

THEIR

Use and Abuse.

———•◆•———

A TRUE NARRATIVE.

BY ANN H. TITUS.

1870.

LUNATIC ASYLUMS.

THEIR USE AND ABUSE.

At a time when humanitarians are investigating prison discipline, and the abuses of power therein, it is not amiss to attract attention to those other seclusions where persons are incarcerated, not for crime, but misfortune.

It is not saying too much, to declare that there is not an Insane Asylum in the United States that does not need thorough investigation and reconstruction. It is well known that they are constantly diverted from their avowed use as curative homes for the insane, and made the horrible prisons where the victims of cupidity or malice are hidden, and rendered powerless to thwart base and wicked designs. Actual out and out murder is attended with inconvenience, and the open doors of insane asylums afford a safer mode of sequestration than the grave. ·

Cases are continually occurring where innocent sane men and women are insnared in these dens. What are known as *private* asylums are preferred for these victims; but even the State asylums are prostituted to base purposes, and receive into ward persons on the representation of only interested parties. Within the past year a lady, resident of Brooklyn, the wife of a New York merchant, being in the way of her husband's *liaison* with another woman, a servant in her house, was, under pretense of a trip to Saratoga, inveigled into Utica Asylum; and admitted there, too, without the prescribed legal formalities having been fully complied with.

The case of Commodore Meade is one of more recent date, and need only be referred to, to recall the motives which induced his imprisonment, which arose, not from his insanity, but the desire of his family to remove a hinderance to his daughter's marriage.

The law provides that certain investigations, legal and medical, shall take place before a person is confined in an insane asylum; but this is constantly evaded or defied. The State can, and does in a great measure, prevent abuse of the State institutions; but the private asylums are frequently made use of unworthily. In these places, *for a price*, persons are continually received without the least form of investigation, or on the *bought* certificates of physicians. It is a blot on the humanity of our people and our lawgivers, that all private insane asylums are not abolished. They are neither more nor less than idiot factories. The moment a sane person is confined in one of these places, it becomes the obvious interest of the proprietors of the retreat to render the victim *insane* as soon as possible.

And it is not uncharitable to conclude, that men unprincipled enough to admit and keep sane persons will be vile enough to try almost everything for the purpose of making a reality of the terrible sham.

One case out of the many comparatively secluded ones now demands attention. It has been hushed up by parties interested in its suppression; but the woman who has suffered misconstruction, deception, and abuse absolutely refuses to keep silence any longer. Her case should be made public, if only for the sake of others now enduring secretly the injustice which she has experienced; and she has, also, her own interests at stake. It does not become any one to bear through life a suspicion never merited, if by any possible means they can make the truth known; so Mrs. Ann H. Titus, in justice to herself and to humanity, feels called upon to give the world a full and exact statement (corroborated by proof of the strongest kind) of her condition and attendant circumstances at the time she was reported insane.

She had lived for years happily with her husband, had

borne him six children, given them the fondest care, and in every way proven herself a worthy wife, good mother, and first-rate housekeeper. The comfort of those years was, however, somewhat interfered with by her husband's parents, who resided with them, and who had the unhappy faculty of making themselves extremely disagreeable to those with whom they were thrown in constant contact. Their daughter-in-law, Ann, became a kind of scape-goat. Being a good Christian woman, Mrs. Titus bore with their ebullitions patiently ; and in this manner her life progressed until the year 1864. Her husband, although at heart a good, conscientious man, was—well, *pliable.* He had none of what Josh Billings styles "*backbone,*" and possessing a character easily managed by those he was with, suffered not only himself from his vacillation, but brought his wife into perilous plans. Like many persons of his stamp, however, Mr. Titus could be firm enough in some directions. His attachment to the house they occupied was very great, and he firmly and persistently refused to invest money in a new building. The house was an old colonial building, over two hundred years of age. Situated on low ground, it was damp and unwholesome. The spaces between the walls were so filled in with the ordure of rats, that in wet or hot weather the stench was almost intolerable. Pig-sties close to the house, rendering matters still worse with the reek of rotting straw. In the rainy weather, the house roof leaking so that pans full of water were caught in the kitchen. Mrs. Titus, never very rugged, in the lapse of years, worn with the heavy work of a farmer's house and the bearing, nursing, and rearing of six children, grew still more fragile, and feeling the imperative need of change, and knowing that with her help their circumstances had altered during the years they had lived together, so as to warrant it, desired a new house. And hearing that a farm. owned by her brother-in-law, Robert R. Willetts, and occupied by his son, was for sale, endeavored to persuade her husband to buy it.

Robert Willetts's wife, Lydia, objected strenuously to the contemplated purchase, for what reason God alone knows. Mrs. Titus insisted on the purchase, and finding that in this case Greek had met Greek, Lydia Willetts determined upon a course, at thought of which a genuine Greek would blush. She went to work systematically enough. A little seed sown here, another there, and soon the harvest—a rumor of Mrs. Titus's insanity—appeared. Not a strange word or action was cited as evidence of this condition ; and even after being conveyed to the asylum, no one was able to bring forward anything in her conversation or demeanor which evidenced lunacy. Unaware of Lydia Willetts's work, Jacob Conklin, the brother of Mrs. Titus, anxious to do her a service, proceeded to purchase for her the farm in question ; and after making the purchase, hearing this report of her insanity, concluded to keep it for his eldest son. How he was induced to believe the story concocted by artful schemers on both sides of the house, Mrs. Titus has never yet discovered ; but that he *did* believe it is self-evident ; and from that time forward he was the most persistent among those who hunted her down.

At this time Mrs. Titus's health was very poor, and she had been recommended change of air by competent physicians. One day she overheard the fragment of a conversation between Jacob Conklin and her mother, in which he exclaimed very excitedly : "Keep her home ! Keep her home ! They say she's crazy." This was the first intimation she had received of her own madness.

Now began the reports concerning her insanity, and they finally came to her knowledge, and were traced to their authors. She at once invited examination into her mental state, and agreed to submit to the decision of the family physician. Dr. Ely, then of Westbury, and now of

White Plains, was called in by Mrs. Titus herself, and asked for a certificate of insanity. And she stated her willingness, if really insane, to go to Bloomingdale. This certificate he utterly refused to give, as he considered Mrs. Titus perfectly sane, though worn by anxiety, and in delicate health. He also stated that she needed rest and change.

I have visited Dr. Ely to learn from him personally his view of this case. He told me, that, in his opinion, Mrs. Titus had never been insane ; he had seen her in times of great excitement and trial, but he had never seen anything in her manner or conduct that betokened insanity. Dr. Ely also gave similar testimony in Court, when, subsequent to her release from Sandford Hall, Mrs. Titus sued Dr. Barstow, Jacob Conklin, and others, for her abduction and incarceration.

Feeling seriously the drafts these trials were making upon her health, and finding her brother determined not to accede to her wishes regarding the property, Mrs. Titus now proposed to take a trip to Norfolk, Va. Before making this arrangement, however, she determined to make one more effort to induce her brother to change his determination regarding the property, and for this purpose she visited him at his place of business. He was very much excited and annoyed, and angry at her persistence, and repeated to her the reports concerning her insanity. Finding the effort with him useless, she proceeded to call upon Dr. Post at Staten Island.

This interview was as unsatisfactory as the former one.

Much discouraged, Mrs. Titus returned home, and made her arrangements to take her journey south. This was in the fall of 1865. Her friends made very little, if any, opposition to this proposed journey, and it was arranged that her daughter, a young girl of seventeen, should accompany her. With this child, who should have been one-hearted with the mother who bore her, the enemy tampered, and she consented to assist in betraying her mother into their hands. In order to do this more effectually, she expressed a desire to stop at her uncle Jacob's, in Williamsburg, while she did some shopping for the journey. In consideration of the bitter feeling between herself and her brother and sister-in-law, Mrs. Titus would have preferred not going to their house, but to accommodate this daughter, her oldest and dearly loved child, she consented, little dreaming that the child she had suffered for, nursed, and tenderly reared was turned against her. It is due to this girl here to state, that however reprehensible her conduct was, she now declares the whole procedure to have been unjustifiable. She was little more than a child, and the designing relatives understood thoroughly how to make her believe in her mother's insanity ; she is now a faithful and affectionate daughter, bitterly sorry for the injustice she once did her dearest friend.

The visit was made. Jacob Conklin announced his intention to accompany them as far as Philadelphia. Soon after getting into the carriage which was to convey them to the boat, Mr. Conklin dropped the blinds, but Mrs. Titus suspected no sinister design until they had been some time on the way ; when, raising the blind and looking out, she saw they had struck the Flushing turnpike. She then remembered there was an asylum there, and the fear struck her that foul play was intended, but she said nothing till they entered the village ; then she said to her daughter : "Maria, thy Uncle Jacob is taking me to an asylum." Jacob said nothing ; but the girl replied : "Oh no, mother, I guess not." When they halted in front of Sandford Hall, she again said : "Maria, this is an asylum." Again Maria responded : "I guess not, mother ; but if it is, I will stay with thee." She had her mother's watch and purse, and now Mrs. Titus asked for them. She refused to give them, saying : " Thee must ask Uncle Jacob," Jacob Conklin now invited her to alight and go to the house and warm herself; this she refused. He then went to the house, and after some moments, returned, and again urged her to go ; the servant who accompanied them, now went in, and came back, saying, there was a nice fire ; then the daughter went in, accompanied by her uncle and the servant. Mrs. Titus now looked out of the carriage, and seeing the coachman had left the horses standing unfastened and alone, thought, perhaps, if she could get to the street, she might, perhaps, persuade her brother to reconsider his course, and either take her home, or allow her to proceed on her journey. She therefore sprang from the carriage, and ran swiftly toward the street. Her brother was soon at her side, and, grasping her arm, said : " Thee must go in here." " I will not go," said she ; "I told thee before, if thee could get a proper certificate of my insanity, I would go to an asylum, and I will do so yet, but I will not go in here." "Thee must," said he ; "Dr. Post says thee must, to keep thee from thinking so much about the farm." " I will not go one step," said the brave woman ; "it shall not be said, I went of my own accord." Then this brother, assisted by others, carried her into the Hall.

The reader will observe, no person in authority came out to see who this woman was ; who, not so insane but what she could be left alone in the carriage, with the horses unattended and unfastened, while her brother and child went into the house, was yet forcibly carried into the house. The only person who came out to meet her was an Irish girl, employed as a nurse in the institution. She was taken into the house, and detained there ; seen by no one belonging to the institution, save the servants, until long after the departure of her relatives. This brother and this daughter left her there alone, taking away with them her watch and purse, and the trunk containing her clothing. Imagine the terrible situation of this delicate invalid, whose nerves were already strained almost to their utmost tension. Betrayed basely ; left in a place from which there was no way of escape ; a prisoner ; it seems almost marvelous that reason was not hurled from its throne. Were such a consummation desired, any better method could hardly be found. She was carried in by the back gateway, through a dismal hall, and put into a comfortless room to await the coming of the Doctor. Two women were here to watch her. Grace, the Irish servant, alluded to above, and another woman. The entertainment afforded this newly made prisoner, was the privilege of hearing said Irish woman read an account of the terrible sufferings of the prisoners at Andersonville. Excellent and judicious treatment for a person supposed to be insane ! Later in the evening she was taken to the "wing" of the building, and put in an up-stairs room, poorly furnished. The bed was uncomfortable ; but Mrs. Titus was so weary, that she thought she should fall asleep at once. Not so, however. The pillow, full of lumpy feathers, bearing evidence of having been wet, was so impregnated with the odor of opium, that the first inhalation of it set her coughing, and she slept none at all. Whether the opium had been placed there for the benefit of this patient in particular, or had been used for some former inmate, or was a part of the curative process used indiscriminately with all who entered this place, we do not know ; but there is no doubt of the fact of the presence of opium.

On the Doctor's return, Mrs. Titus told him her case ; the family difficulties, and the jealousy arising about the farm, which was the reason of her being placed in this position. He remarked, that she was much worn down, and needed bracing up. She told him yes ; but that she was not insane. He expressed to her no opinion on the subject, but said he was sorry he had not been there when her brother left her, for he had no suitable room for her. The expression of his face was troubled, and he seemed to deprecate the action of Mrs. Titus's friends.

The next morning, when Dr. Barstow came to visit her, she said to him : "Doctor, I told thee last night I was not a fit subject for an asylum ; but, I think, this way I soon shall be."

"Did you not sleep, Mrs. Titus ?"

"Not a wink," she replied.

He then called to the woman who attended that ward. "Did not Mrs. Titus sleep last night ?" "No, sir, not at all ; she coughed all night, and was so disturbed during the early part of the night by the talking of a patient in the adjoining room, that, had she not so suffered, sleep would have been impossible." Mrs. Titus then spoke of the wrong done her in keeping her there, and of the injustice done her by those who put her there. The Doctor answered rather cavalierly, that he guessed they knew what they were about. "Why, Doctor," said she, "Dr. Ely says if one is crazy they most always know it." The Doctor answered : "Always ;" and repeated it with emphasis, "*always.*" "Then," said Mrs. Titus, "I am not insane ; for I know I am not." All day the bustle and noise in the department continued so incessantly that any repose was impossible ; and Mrs. Titus, already worn and weak with ill health, felt the effect it was having on her nervous system. In the afternoon it became more quiet, but still she slept but little. That night the Doctor prescribed a *quieting* potion for her, which only increased her suffering and wakefulness. She had hardly swallowed it, when her ears were filled with strange noises, like swarming of bees, shrill steam whistlings, rumbling as of thunder, and such distress, that it seemed as if congestion of the brain was inevitable. Accustomed to homœopathic treatment, this allopathic heroic usage was too much for her. This night, however, she got some sleep. It seems very strange, and is a fact that should be known, that it was generally understood by Mrs. Titus's family and friends that she could not endure the allopathic treatment. They often said among themselves that she would die under such a *regime*, that homœopathic treatment was the only kind she could bear. Yet here she was placed in an asylum where they *knew* she would be subjected to the very course which they themselves declared would be death to her. They were quite aware, too, that she was compelled to take medicine which affected her so powerfully that she feared, with good cause, not only for her reason, but her life. Yet they left her there to suffer.

We stated above, that her clothes had been taken back in the carriage. She supposed that this was because her own and her daughter's had been packed together, and they wished to separate them. She found, however, that such was not the case. She received her clothes six days after her arrival, during that time having no change of raiment, having no wrapper to lie down in ; ill and suffering, it was uncomfortable, indeed, to recline in the traveling dress she wore. When her clothes arrived they were in a small portmanteau, insufficient in quantity, and gathered from her poorest and oldest clothes. The only thick dress sent her was a light merino, which she had had for thirteen years. Her furs, which she much needed, she was not allowed to have for weeks ; nor was a wrapping gown sent her until the 18th inst. Not only were her friends unjust to her, but neglectful and cruel. The blame should not rest upon the daughter too heavily, for no responsibility had ever been hers ; she had never yet made a garment for herself, and perhaps did not appreciate the needs of her mother for warm and comfortable clothes.

It is to be remembered here, that Mrs. Titus's husband

did not know of her incarceration at the time of it, nor of the intention on the part of her brother to imprison her ; but knowing her health to be delicate, he was persuaded by the family (remember Jacob Conklin's wife was his own sister) that she would recruit as well under treatment there, as by a journey to Norfolk. Dr. Barstow, the physician at Sandford Hall, was placed, during the first days of Mrs. Titus's confinement, in rather a predicament. He did not know how far Mr. Titus might consent to the will of his brother, and not until the tenth day after her arrival, did the Doctor and husband meet. Up to this date Mrs. Titus's unpleasant symptoms had been steadily increasing, her sleep becoming more and more disturbed, and the effect of the medicine given more unpleasant. From this date, on which the Doctor learned from Mr. Titus, and perhaps persuaded him to, his consent to Mrs. Titus's continued stay at Sandford Hall, her treatment was more severe, and the effect of the medicine more marked. This increased till the fourth week, when the powerful medicines, evidently some combination of opium and iron, and always administered when the patient's stomach was empty, that is, about midway between the meals, and just before retiring, affected her so powerfully, that for five days and nights she never slept one moment. It is needless to tell medical men what the effect of these drugs, administered in this way, would be ; needless to hint that Dr. Barstow must have known what the tendency of this treatment must be ; or to suggest to the popular mind that it was for his interest and that of the man who placed her there, that this patient should be rendered really insane. Five sleepless nights and days would render many a sane and pretty strong-nerved person maniacal. But God sustained this poor victim to confound her enemies. And she will deem her sufferings but a light affliction, if so be those in power may be led to look into these things, and make provision to protect women against their protectors, and abolish these iniquitous idiot factories, by punishing not only persons who unlawfully entomb them, but the physicians who will lend their aid by signing certificates of the insanity of persons without the legal formulas, and oftentimes without even having seen the accused. And the keepers of these places, who receive into their charge persons so victimized. To prove that this treatment did not overthrow Mrs. Titus's reason it is well to state here, that the day after these five sleepless nights, Mrs. Barstow invited Mrs. Titus into the library to meet some of the inmates and guests, preparing a tree for Christmas. In her weak state, Mrs. Titus went down stairs and sat for awhile ; but feeling overcome and faint, found strength to regain her room, and just as she was recovering from her attack, Mrs. Eliza H. McDonald, Mrs. Barstow's mother, came in and conversed for nearly an hour with her. If Mrs. Titus's mind was at any time deranged, this would have been the time for the fact to be seen. But Mrs. McDonald testified afterward in Court, that at no time did she see any particular signs of insanity. During all those nights of agony no nurse was in Mrs. Titus's apartment, when she so much needed bathing, rubbing, and soothing treatment to induce sleep, not a single thing was ordered or done to that ultimate. Does this look as if a *curative* process was intended?

On this sixth day Mrs. Titus received from home a package containing her furs and a dress, and in with the furs a couple of bottles of homœopathic medicine—ipecac and pulsatilla—which, knowing her mother to be in the habit of taking, she supposed she might want. That night she left Dr. Barstow's medicine standing and took her homœopathic pellets. Whether it was the effect of not taking the allopathic medicine, or the effect of taking the homœopathic, that night she slept. The next day Mrs. Titus said to the chambermaid : "Eliza, I do not wish this medicine, leave it there and I will tell the Doctor." Eliza, however, either returned the medicine or threw it away, and the Doctor knew nothing of it for several days.

During this period, Mrs. Titus's health improved so rapidly that she lost much of her repugnance to being at the Hall, it was such a comfort to be free of the terrible suffering. On the seventh night, however, as Mrs. Titus was up late and there had been considerable excitement with the Christmas festivities, she took a dose of opium which the Doctor prescribed, saying it would make her sleep better. This was simple opium, without the iron—and, on this night, as on the five nights preceding the sixth night, she lost her rest. Then she determined to take as little as possible of the medicine given her, and had she been as prudent as Eliza, and said nothing to the Doctor, she might have gone on improving, in spite of prescriptions, which, in her case at least, were poisonous. However, she was so pleased to find her condition changing for the better, that, seeing how much interest the Doctor professed in her case, she told him frankly that she had made the experiment of doing without his medicine, and found herself better. He seemed to treat the matter lightly at first, and laughed at her ideas of homœopathy—but finding her thoroughly convinced that she was right, and determined to pursue her own course, he began threatening to compel her to take his nostrums. Still, by persuasion, she was enabled for some time to have the doses reduced in quantity, and taking her own ipecacuanha which is an antidote for the other medicines, she was enabled to keep pretty well for seventeen days. During this time there was considerable excitement in the house, both among the patients and employees, concerning Mrs. Titus's aversion to the course she was subjected to, and Dr. Barstow seemed very much discontented and chagrined, for it was quite evident that Mrs. Titus was improving both in health and spirits. All the inmates evinced much pleasure at her return to strength and health.

At the end of about two weeks from the time Mrs. Titus commenced taking her own medicine it began to fail, and she asked the Doctor to request her friends to send her a new supply. This he refused to do ; upon which Mrs. Titus declared : " Then I will not take thine." The Doctor made no reply, but turned angrily away, and in less than five minutes was driving toward the city. Now what follows ? In the short time intervening between his interview with his patient and his departure for New York, he has given his orders to the servants concerning Mrs. Titus. Let it here be stated that the word servant is used *advisedly,* for there were no *nurses* in Sandford Hall. There was no assistant resident physician—Dr. Ogden visited the establishment once a week, and sometimes saw the patients and sometimes *not.* Observe here, Dr. Barstow was away in the city two days in the week—Tuesdays and Saturdays—should any patient be taken ill during this absence, there was no physician, professed nurse, nor any person in the house competent to act advisedly in the case. This in an asylum where $30 a week was not thought too much for board and medical attendance ! The matron, Miss Benedict, acted as housekeeper merely, seldom being seen among the patients except at table. The only time in which Mrs. Titus knew her to act in any degree in capacity of nurse was on an occasion when she carried a wine sling to a patient in spasms.

Shortly after the Doctor's departure, Mrs. Titus left the sitting-room and went to her own room. It was a damp and rather drizzly day, and having occasion to go into the yard she changed her dress, putting on the old merino, intending to change it as soon as she came in, that she might not take cold, her delicate state of health rendering her extremely susceptible to the changes of weather. As she came in she met Grace, the big Irish woman before alluded to, who said : "Mrs. Titus, come up in the wing and see Mrs. Lewis." "May be the Doctor would not like it," said Mrs. Titus. "Oh yes," answered Grace, "the Doctor said you were to go." Mrs. Titus suspecting nothing, followed Grace to the wing, which, the reader will please remember, was the part of the house devoted to unruly and incurable cases, they entered the sitting-room and while Mrs. Titus was conversing with Ann, who remarked that Mrs. Lewis was engaged just then having her hair combed, and asked Mrs. Titus to wait awhile, Grace left the room, returning shortly with a wine-glass of medicine which she placed on the table, and turning to Mrs. Titus said : " Now you must take it, Mrs. Titus, the Doctor says you must." Mrs. Titus saw at once the siutation, and, throwing up her hands, exclaimed : "Oh, Grace !" It seemed to her now that the climax was come. The shock of this was worse even than that of being taken to the Hall. Grace said : "Well, you must take it." "Oh, Grace, it is an awful dose," said Mrs. Titus. And on her still further refusal, she grew angry and calling on her fellow-servant to help her, poured the medicine down while Ann held Mrs. Titus. She swallowed only part of it, upon which Ann held Mrs. Titus's nose, forcing her to swallow the remainder. Weak, and shocked, and tired as she was, she was almost immediately ordered into an adjoining room, which was cold, and, having a window open, was also damp. The excuse given for this was, that Ann, the chambermaid of that wing, wanted to sweep the sitting-room. Shortly she came in and began to complain of having another patient to take care of ; but as she talked, her tone changed, and from complaints of her own inconvenience she went to pitying Mrs. Titus, saying she

did not know what she would do there. "Thee remembers
I was here five days and nights before, doesn't thee?" said
Mrs. Titus. "Oh, yes," observed the woman, who, when
Mrs. Titus had been at the wing before, was as kind and
attentive as was in her power. "Well, God brought me
out of here then, and he will bring me out of Sandford Hall
now." The woman looked rather struck by the firm way
in which Mrs. Titus spoke, and very soon went down stairs ;
returning, she told Mrs. Titus she could go down stairs
again. To this Mrs. Titus, who felt at this time peculiarly
the presence of the divine Spirit sustaining and strength-
ening her, replied : "I am beginning to feel I could be
happy up here ;" but having the liberty, she went down,
and at the foot of the stairs met Grace, who said :
"Remember, Mrs. Titus, you must take the medicine," and
repeated it. Mrs. Titus answered her : "I will take it,
since I must, but I shall consider it always as a poisoned
dose." Then Grace allowed her to pass, and she returned
to the sitting-room, which was occupied by Miss Judd,
who was a sort of assistant matron. Mrs. Titus re-
strained herself from making any complaint to her concerning the ordeal she had been subjected to, regarding
the order of Dr. Barstow, for the moment, as the passion-
ate freak of an undisciplined boy, rather than the deliberate, cruel mandate of a man of power. Nor did she
yet suspect that the dose, though rather larger than usual,
was more powerful in quality. She exercised some with
the patients in the hall, and then entered into conversation with Miss Judd. While talking with her, she felt a
very unpleasant burning sensation in the stomach, and
mentioning the fact to her, without relating the cause,
asked for some bread and butter, which she at once ob-
tained. This quieted the symptoms somewhat ; and when
it was proposed to visit the Library and get a book to read,
she went down, and after some searching for one to suit,

selected *Lady Huntington and her Friends ;* before, however, she had read much, she was seized with great distress ; burning and sickness at the stomach. She went to her room and vomited violently ; her stomach, at the time, being almost empty, the straining was violent, and what she raised was tinged with blood.

The Doctor returned that evening, and spoke to Mrs. Titus from the hall, saying he had seen her brother. She answered, saying, she did not wish to hear about him. He passed on, not entering the room or making any inquiry as to her health. The next morning he came in, and asked how she did. Her answer was : " As well, Doctor, as thee could expect, after the dose of poison thee ordered poured down." At this he flushed up angrily, and said : " Now, Mrs. Titus, I think you had better go and stay with Grace. You have made disturbance enough in the house, talking about poison, and you've been giving Eliza (one of the maids) homœopathic medicine too." " Yes," she replied ; " I believe I gave her three pellets ;" which was the case. Eliza was subject to some headaches which the Doctor failed to cure. Mrs. Titus gave her, on one of these occasions, three pellets, as stated, and Eliza declared they relieved her. Mrs. Titus told the Doctor she had no dislike to him, or Mrs. McDonald, or any of them, but she was convinced that the medicine did not agree with her, and that, in her case, given in such strength and quantity, it was no less than poison. He then spoke of calling in Dr. Post, who was also a physician of the old school, and influenced by Jacob Conklin, as before stated. He sent in more medicine, too, as soon as he left, which, of course, she was obliged to take. After taking it, the same burning sensation she had before experienced set in, accompanied with oppression of the chest, and such difficulty of breathing, that Kate and Miss Judd were attracted to her room by the sound of her labored respiration.

She asked them to put a wet cloth on her chest, which they did, and then she asked for something to eat, knowing from experience that it would alleviate her symptoms, and mentioned several things . which she would like. They shortly went down stairs, and she was left alone ; no one came near her ; no food was sent up ; dinner-time came and passed ; still no relief. About three o'clock, after dinner, Eliza came up, and sitting down, said : "Well, Mrs. Titus, what about your dinner ?" "I do not know," said she ; "I suspect the Doctor does not intend me to have any." Those who have never suffered from inflammation of the stomach can hardly imagine the acute sufferings she endured, but any physician will perceive the effect of such stimulating doses upon the stomach and system of a patient in a weak and exhausted condition, who is kept fasting or on a low diet ; and they can also judge what the effect of such treatment would be on the mental condition of a person supposed to be insane, or in imminent danger of insanity. Physicians should know also, that where there is violent inflammation of the digestive · organs, unless emollient food is given, great danger to the brain exists. It is scarcely to be supposed that Dr. Barstow could have been so deplorably ignorant, as not to know the legitimate result of such treatment as he was subjecting Mrs. Titus to. Nor does it seem an insane or illogical conclusion for his victim to arrive at, that he was employed and encouraged by the brother who put her there, and whom he had seen the previous day, to induce that result. Mrs. Titus told the Doctor herself, early in her stay there, that she feared effusion of water on the brain from her suffering. He said : "Oh, no, it was only congestion," yet he gave her iron and opium in large doses, and on an empty stomach.

Mrs. Titus, let it here be understood, had never been troubled in this manner before. So that it is self-evident that her strange sickness was caused by this Doctor's ignorant (or malicious) treatment. ·

There seems good reason to suspect that he intended she should have been kept in the wing the day she was sent there to take that dose. The servants acknowledged that, in allowing her to go down, they were disobeying duties. Had she stayed up there she might as well have been in a cell, for the transactions of that part of the house were kept to itself. The assistant matrons did not visit it. The idiots, incurables, and rebellious were there, and only the Doctor and the servants, who had charge of that department, entered it. The simple facts are given, let the reader come to what conclusions he will.

Mrs. Titus's suspicions were aroused the very first night of her stay in Sandford Hall, by something she overheard, that the place was not an insane asylum, only taking patients for so much a week to board and cure them, but that it was also a prison in which, for a price paid, any person might be incarcerated so long as the nursery was found to pay the price. From this time out she kept a strict watch on all the machinery of the institution, carefully and prudently questioning the inmates, both patients and employees, and comparing what she heard with what she saw. That her conclusions were not far from right, the history of her stay there, and subsequent events clearly show. (That the charge, that it is an idiot factory, and a fiery furnace.)

Mrs. Titus waited in vain for dinner; it was Sunday, and after service, that Miss Judd came through the hall, and Mrs. Titus, who was suffering in an agony of fever and pain, so that, weak as she was, she was obliged to get up and walk to relieve the terrible pain which resulted from the use of medicine that had inflamed the mucous membrane of the stomach to an agonizing degree, went to the door and asked her to bring her some food.

Miss Judd, who was always kind, went at once herself and made toast and brought it up. This, as usual, had an alleviating effect, and at teatime a couple of buns, afterward some arrow-root was sent up; weak, and only about a teacupful in quantity. From the fact, that neither Miss Judd nor Kate, both of whom Mrs. Titus knew to be kindly disposed, did not come to her room of their own accord, Mrs. Titus concluded that the Doctor had prohibited their so doing, and weeks afterward was informed that her idea was correct. What object he could have had in leaving her to suffer thus solitarily, let the reader imagine. Nor did the Doctor himself visit her from Sunday morning until Monday evening, when he evidently was somewhat frightened at the thoroughness of his work, and wrote immediately for Dr. Post to come up. Mrs. Titus had no arrow-root after Sunday night. Monday morning her breakfast consisted of some bread dipped in milk and water, her dinner of beef-tea, and her supper again of the same sort as her breakfast. When the Doctor came up, he asked her about her appetite and food, and she told him the insufficiency of it; and he asked her how she would like oysters, she said she would like them; and the next morning some were sent up, but insufficiently cooked, so that she could not relish them. There was no person in the establishment whose duty it was to cook and arrange the delicate dishes needed for invalids. Dr. Barstow gave the orders, if anything especial was needed; and no one being appointed to see to it, the invalid's meal was apt to be served in the manner above stated. The dinners served were generally good in quantity and quality, but not such as invalids like Mrs. Titus require.

The Tuesday following the severe attack above spoken of, the dinner served to her was *corned* beef. The breakfasts and suppers were insufficient. So that taking it altogether, not only this especial invalid, but others suffered for want of proper nourishment. What excuse can be given for this in an institution like Sandford Hall, where no boarders are taken except at high prices? Nothing, it is well-known, is more important to mental health than particular attention to general dietary and physical laws. The bill of fare at Sandford Hall was good enough in some respects, and generally the dinners were excellent ; but the breakfasts, while occasionally good, were too often of a sort from which an invalid, like Mrs. Titus, could select nothing suitable, save milk and water, and bread. In her condition she needed constant nourishing diet ; a single meal missed was a serious detriment to her, and she felt the effects keenly, not only at the time, but for days afterward ; and she knew that every retrograde step only made her condition more and more doubtful. An insufficient breakfast of the sort above named, and a dinner of corned beef, or rich poultry, neither of which she could eat. With supper of toast and tea, and perhaps rich cake, which was equally as unsuited to her as the corned beef, did not leave her a very large bill of fare from which to select suitable diet.

During all this week, Mrs. Titus, as said, was kept alone. Dr. Post came and did not prohibit the Doctor's course, but gave quinine to break the chills which accompanied the fever. It can easily be understood how Dr. Post was influenced. He is the cousin of Jacob Conklin's wife, and consequently of Mr. William Titus. He had recommended, so says Jacob Conklin, that Mrs. Titus should be shut up to keep her from thinking so much about the farm. They had so done, and now he must stand by his own standard, he must defend the position of Jacob Conklin—he must suppose Mrs. Titus crazy, or show up Jacob Conklin in the character of a designing scoundrel, and himself as his counselor. Perhaps, too, he did think Mrs. Titus a little unbalanced ; and if she was, what harm in making her enough more so to make it patent to all beholders ? What even if she were made as others had been made before her, *idiotic ?* Why would not the course of Jacob Conklin, Dr. Post & Co., be therein plausibly vindicated ? We know many medical men are ignorant in these matters, but Dr. Post has no such excuse. A disciple of Dr. Mott, for many years a physician in the employ of one of the largest Life Insurance Companies in the country, and ranking high in his profession, he yet allowed himself to be drawn into a family difficulty, and into partnership with " *his side of the house,*" as to doom this woman to abduction, incarceration, and slow poison. Mrs. Titus begged Dr. Post to order the continuance of the homœopathic ipecacuanha ; this he declined to do, saying it interfered with Dr. Barstow's medicine. The reader will please remember this acknowledgment, and also, while taking the ipecac, Mrs. Titus was relieved of the terrible suffering she endured from the Doctor's medicine. However, he consented at length to prescribe it, and also, at her request, prescribed potassium, which she found so strong that she could scarcely take it. Remember, they say she was crazy, yet they sent this crazy woman potassium in such strength that had she taken it she must have died.

A few days after this, Dr. Barstow left Sandford Hall, on a journey of four or five days, and Dr. Ordenan took his place ; this, at such a critical period in Mrs. Titus's case, was indeed providential. Mrs. Titus did not tell him her suspicions, nor the ordeal she had been subjected to, but he entered into her views of the case. Dr. Barstow had left strict directions with Kate that the medicine he had prescribed should not be changed, but administered to Mrs. Titus as usual, not leaving it to Dr. Ordenan's judgment to discontinue it, so the iron and opium were administered as usual. Dr. Ordenan said that ipecac and pulsatilla or bryonia homœopathically administered would be just the thing for her. Seeing the tumbler with the potassium on the table by Mrs. Titus's bed, so placed that she might take it in the night, he tasted it, and immediately spit it out and asked for water to rinse his mouth, saying : " Mrs. Titus, you don't take this, do you ? It is strong enough to eat your stomach up." Before Barstow returned, Mrs. Titus begged him to give her some extra opium powders ; he at first declined, saying Barstow would give them as she needed them ; she replied : " I don't know about that, Dr. Ordenan, a burned child dreads the fire ;" and he made her up some, for which she had reason to be thankful, for when Barstow returned he almost every other time put acetate of iron into the ipecac, which burnt her almost like cayenne pepper, and counteracted the effect of the ipecacuanha. It seemed as if he was determined to effect her insanity. Mrs. Titus now began to understand that the effect of the medicine was rendered less unbearable if she took it just after eating, and ate again very soon after taking it ; therefore, when her meals were brought up, she saved all that she could spare from each meal, rich cake, or meat, or what not, and secreting it, kept it for these occasions, and soon found the benefit of it. Her close observation of her own case, her insight into the incentives she knew existed in her brother's mind to urge him to keep her there, the disgrace and discomfiture that would accrue to a large number of intermarried relatives, and the damage it would be to the institution if she should walk out of it sane and well, and expose its machinery, made her understand more fully the reason why it was to the Doctor's interest, as well as Mr. Conklin's, to keep her there.

After the inmates of the asylum had all retired, somewhere between the hours of ten and two, the *honorable* Dr. Barstow would examine the letters Mrs. Titus had written friends outside. Now, why should a respectable physician, in a respectable institution, care what one of his patients chose to write? If all correspondence had been vetoed utterly, the proceeding could scarcely be considered justifiable, the missives might then have been burned without examination ; but why one should be allowed to go, and another withheld, according to the ideas of Dr. Barstow, is more than we can understand. The ravings of an insane woman would never be heeded by sensible individuals, and the only conclusion left is—that Mrs. Titus's letters were so full of truth as to be dangerous to himself. He directed all her friends to abstain from writing her. Why? And the few who, in the face of this injunction, dared to send the poor oppressed woman words of cheer and comfort, had their missives opened and perused some hours before Mrs. Titus was allowed to read them. They were carefully sealed afterward ; but to the truth of these statements Barstow has himself testified in open court.

During the few days of Dr. Ordenan's stay, Mrs. Titus was sorely tempted to make him her confidant, and reveal the whole disgraceful story ; but upon reflection, she concluded that such an *exposé* might only make a bad matter worse. Dr. Barstow would not have been likely to put in such a position any one who would sympathize with her position, even if they believed her story ; so she did not even disclose the fact that they *forced* her to take the medicine, which was in his opinion " strong enough to eat her stomach up." This physician treated her with far more consideration than she had received during her stay at the Hall, and it was sorrowfully enough she saw him take his departure.

Dr. Barstow's fiendish disposition had not altered for the better during his short absence. Upon his return he commenced his persecutions with redoubled vigor, apparently supplied with new diabolisms. The distasteful doses were continued, and everything went on as before. About this time, at the suggestion of Dr. Post, of Staten Island, who co-operated fully with Dr. B. and designing relatives, her husband and eldest daughter (the one instrumental in effecting her incarceration), paid her a visit. She was looking haggard and pale, being really very ill, and the wily physician concluded that this would be a favorable opportunity of having her so-called insanity proven. Like many villains, he overshot his mark, for to this visit Mrs. Titus doubtless owed her ultimate release. Her husband said he was very much surprised at the underhand means employed to convey her to the asylum, and vehemently disclaimed any complicity in the business. Doubtless he was innocent, but like many others of his calibre, he did not choose to make a bad matter worse by useless repining ; so, imagining her comfortable, settled phlegmatically down, thinking that as others had taken the responsibility so far, he would allow them to retain it without interference. This visit, however, opened his eyes to many things. He was not a stupid man, and although his wife was too ill to complain, he saw that her confinement had been anything but beneficial—that instead of improving, her health had retrograded ; and Mr. Titus took his departure, very much more worried than he chose to confess. The daughter, although visibly shocked at her mother's emaciated appearance, tried to appear cheerful, and to this end praised her surroundings enthusiastically. Mrs. Titus had neither the strength nor desire to reproach the child for her share in what—had the villainous machinations been successful—would have proven a terrible tragedy, and her silence did far more than any words could have done. Mr. Titus after this visit called upon Dr. Post, to discuss the expediency of taking her away. This model physician interposed every objection, cursing, doubtless, his own stupidity in advising the visit, which had resulted thus disastrously to all their plans. But finally Mr. Titus became suspicious of and indignant at his continued opposition, and expressed his determination of taking her to Norfolk just as soon as the weather moderated, with or without permission. Both Dr. Barstow and Dr. Post represented the insanity of Mrs. Titus as being of a very mild type, not at all dangerous, and why in the name of heaven were they so opposed to her taking a journey which they knew would benefit her physically, and could not affect her mentally except for the better?

After Mr. Titus's exhibition of will—a will which neither physician gave him credit for possessing—they thought it prudent to modify their position a little, so very reluctantly gave their consent to the proposed removal. Well did they know that their proceedings would not stand the test of a close examination ; and well, too, did they know that if Mr. Titus should discover the twentieth part of the truth, their little game would be up, and forever. So, in order to lull his suspicions, they consented to the removal, intending that if science, cunning, and wickedness availed anything, the consent might just as well not have been given. Neither had the slightest idea of allowing their victim to leave Sandford Hall.

When Mr. Titus was at the asylum Dr. Barstow gave him permission to write his wife, although she was not to respond ; but after his visit was concluded, this changeable disciple of Esculapius retracted this permission ; and fearful of Mrs. Titus's being eventually taken from the asylum, Dr. Barstow determined upon weakening her, body and mind, so that any change would be impossible. This determination Mrs. Titus perceived in the increased acerbity of his manner and actions toward her, and more fearful than ever of the unscrupulous man into whose clutches she had been so mercilessly placed, she wrote to her husband begging him to take her away immediately, as she was in constant fear of one of those awful doses to which she had been treated shortly after her arrival. Dr. Barstow did not dare detain this letter. He feared Mr. Titus, and thinking that he could pass off the contents as the delusions of an unsound mind, he allowed it to reach its destination without hindrance. But upon that same evening he gave her the "awful dose" which she had so much reason to dread. After being *coerced* into taking this, Mrs. Titus wrote her husband that her fears had been realized, and inclosed a little piece of cotton saturated with the stuff, to show him what kind of poison was forced into her delicate system. The half sheet of paper to which this piece of cotton was attached Dr. Barstow removed, and the letter, minus the sample, proceeded to its destination. To this, also, he confessed in open court, but excused himself on the ground that it was "a very innocent kind of medicine."

"Very innocent!" It must have been remarkably so! Why, then, did he abstract it? If the "innocent medicine" had been allowed to go on its way, it would have established either his guilt or Mrs. Titus's insanity beyond a peradventure. He must have liked remaining under such a foul suspicion, if he took so much trouble to prevent its being put away. Bah! from his own lips we condemn him; and God grant we may soon see the day when such knaves are deprived of the reins of power, and put in their rightful position.

Now see how cunningly and diabolically the proprietor of Sandford Hall endeavors to counteract the influence of her letters. He writes to Mr. Titus, inclosing the one from his wife, in which she mentions her dread of himself and his concoctions; writes for the ostensible purpose of arranging about her removal, but in reality to do away with any suspicions her missive might raise. Here is his first letter verbatim:

"*February* 10, 1865.

"*My dear Sir:*—I remit inclosed letter from Mrs. Titus. She proposes Thursday, the day already mentioned by Mr. Conklin." [Her brother, who was also consulted concerning her removal.] "If you conclude upon that day, please let me know a day or two before, that we may have everything ready." [The gentleman, like most knaves, disliked surprises. As may be inferred, he wasn't always prepared for visitors ; and in a case like this, where so much was involved, he liked plenty of time for preparation.] "Mrs. Titus is much better in many respects, although far from well." [Very encouraging ; but this little item, although true, occasioned the writer any amount of distress and annoyance. He couldn't account for it. The doses he had insisted upon her taking, since Mr. Titus's announcement · of his determination to remove her from the asylum, had acted very strangely, and their effect was anything but satisfactory. We will explain why Mrs. Titus took the medicine just before retiring. Under her sheet she concealed a napkin, into which she spit the medicine, as soon as the giver turned to replace the bottle in which it was kept.] "For the last two days she has been extremely irritable, which is something I have not noticed before in her case since she has been here. *Her case is a very peculiar one*" [decidedly so] "*and I wish I could speak more encouragingly of her future.* However, we must hope for the best, and I trust she may make the journey with comfort and benefit." [A journey which the hypocrite had firmly decided should never be made.] "I am, dear sir, truly yours,   "J. W. BARSTOW."

This epistle was simply intended to avert suspicion from himself, and it answered admirably. Without stooping to deny any of her charges, or even to notice them, he controverts her whole letter by the expression : "Her case is a very peculiar one." Then Mrs. Titus informs her husband that her "fears have been realized ;" and in order to make that information null and void, Dr. Barstow is obliged to write more definitely, so his next missive is much longer, and far more explicit. It reads thus :

"*My dear Sir:*—You favor of the 13th is received. I am not sure that Mr. Conklin fixed upon the 16th positively" [for Mrs. Titus's removal,] "but my impression is, that he said 'on or about the 16th.' Mrs. Titus received your letter, and writes by this post. The same condition which I described in my last letter continues. Her irritability and restlessness are still extreme." [How could they well be otherwise ?] "And a morbid suspicion of those around her." [This reads rather crudely, but is an exact copy of the original manuscript.] "*Until within the past few days I have not observed any disposition to suspect myself of any sinister purpose;* but she has now conceived the idea that *she is to be poisoned, or injured by medicine.*" [Observe how well he puts it, abstracting, however, the sample of "medicine," which Mrs. Titus inclosed in the identical letter, which he speaks of her as writing. Why did he not allow it to go, so as to show its virtue ?] "She is, indeed, greatly to be pitied, and I doubt the expediency of sending her daughter with her on the proposed trip to Norfolk. The care of her mother in such a condition would be almost too great a responsibility for one so young, and I would suggest that an older person, one of more experience, and more likely to have an influence upon Mrs. Titus, *would be much safer*, and more likely to make the journey a successful one." [Very cunningly put. Every one will perceive that he is gently paving the way for his refusal to allow Mrs. Titus to leave the asylum on the ground of danger.] "The singular change in her temper, and in the general aspect of the case during the few days past, *has discouraged me very much in the hope I indulged a month ago, that Mrs. Titus might be restored.* Still I would not regard it as entirely hopeless, although *I have many fears in regard to the journey.* You have my warmest sympathies, my dear sir, in this very great affliction ; and while I am glad that your poor wife is somewhat better physically than at the time of her coming to us, I only wish I could do more to avert the sad cloud that threatens to settle down upon her reason and her happiness." [Satan himself could not have invented three larger falsehoods in one sentence.] " Whenever you arrange to come for Mrs. Titus, I will have everything in readiness, so that there shall be no detention. *If convenient, please write me a day or two before.*" [So that if his doses (which she did not swallow) had not the desired effect, he could increase or change them, in time to prevent the journey, concerning which he entertained so many fears.] This, with his name and date (February 15th) appended composed the epistle, which, strange to say, did not alter the views of Mr. Titus, concerning the advisability of her removal, at all.

While upon the subject of Dr. Barstow and his letters, it may be as well to copy a very wonderful affair which he wrote to Jacob Conklin, immediately after Mrs. Titus's incarceration. It shows up the business management of Sandford Hall in anything but an agreeable light, and will do more to convince the public of the proprietor's utter heartlessness, and lack of conscience, than anything our indignant soul could possibly dictate. This is the note, word for word :

" *November* 27, 1864.

" *My dear Sir :*—I greatly regret that I was absent yesterday when you brought Mrs. Titus to Sandford Hall, and I am anxious to see you to learn *some particulars of her case.* Will you have the kindness to call at my office in town, No. 4 St. Mark's Place, on Tuesday morning next,

29th inst., between ten and twelve o'clock? Mrs. T. passed a restless night, but has been tolerably calm to-day, and the prospect seems fair that she may have some rest to-night. I will tell you more fully her condition on Tuesday. Do not fail to call. The clothes can be sent by Foster's express office." [This is copied verbatim, and if the reader laughs at the idea of transforming express offices into messengers, let him rest the mistake where it belongs, on Dr. Barstow, not on the transcriber.]

"Truly yours,

"11 *James's Slip.*"   " J. W. Barstow."

Now, it seems simply impossible that such a letter could be written in this nineteenth century by an individual who expected to keep out of Sing Sing. Over his own signature Dr. Barstow has proclaimed himself a villain. What right has he to *admit and treat* Mrs. Titus as a lunatic without "some particulars of her case." And he not only did this, but *worse*. He never even *saw* her until after her imprisonment in his establishment. And without " particulars" from her relatives—without even the farce of an examination by himself, he locked up in his establishment a sane woman, because—he received for it thirty dollars per week. Sandford Hall should be entitled "The Kidnapper's Retreat." It is nothing more nor less, and the whole world should be made aware of the fact.

Notwithstanding the advice of Dr. Barstow, Mr. Titus decided upon having his daughter accompany her mother on the proposed trip to Norfolk. He scarcely credited Barstow's insinuations concerning safety, and the letters of this wily villain only increased his anxiety to get his wife from out of Sandford Hall. Jacob Conklin's behavior was altogether mysterious. Mrs. Titus was his own sister, but judging from his conduct after the reports of her insanity, no one could have believed it. Whether or no he credited these reports is a disputed question. Certain it is, if he did not give them credence, he is a most unnatural brother and depraved man ; while, if they really received his belief, his unhappy credulity can not be too deeply commiserated. Certain it is, he was in league at this time with Dr. Barstow, and was utterly opposed to the idea of having his sister leave the institution over which this scamp presided. Mrs. Titus's daughter at this time was visiting his family. Mr. Titus called, obedient to promise, upon the day fixed upon for them to go and release the poor prisoner, and found his daughter had flown. A wedding some distance off had afforded the uncle an excellent pretext for preventing her proposed trip, and she, being considerably under his influence, had consented to the change of programme. Just at this particular time marriages and deaths were happening in singular promiscuity. The mother of Mrs. Titus had died, and was to be buried on the succeeding day. The wedding party were to attend the funeral ; but expostulation and entreaty were alike lost on Mr. Titus. He would not remain. He had promised his wife to come for her at Sandford Hall at such a date, and he should fulfill that promise if every relative he or she had in the world were to be buried at the same time. If his daughter was away, he would go alone ; but go he would, and did.

So, at the time appointed, he made his appearance in Flushing, with a large carriage and light pillows. Mrs. Titus saw him from her window ; had it not been for that, she might now have been a prisoner. Had he come in the cars, as Dr. Barstow confidently expected, he would have been sent away with the information that his wife was entirely too ill to be seen. But his coming before her window made that explanation impossible, as the lady, knowing the very unscrupulous character of her temporary guardian, hastened before her husband to contradict by her presence any story Dr. Barstow might choose to trump up concerning her illness, unfitness to travel, etc. The Doctor's anxiety at this particular time entirely crushed out his customary caution. He had never imagined the possibility of Mr. Titus's choosing a private carriage for his conveyance, and this fact is not so strange as it may appear. He had good reasons for his apparent carelessness. Mrs. Titus was to go directly to Norfolk. The journey to that city can not be made in a carriage ; and so, acting on these premises, Dr. Barstow prepared himself for probabilities, without giving the slightest heed to possible contingencies. Probably, had the programme been carried out as originally intended, his course would have been sufficiently prudent ; but owing to the absence of his daughter, and other causes which space does not permit us to give, Mr. Titus decided to postpone the journey to Norfolk, and take his wife home. So this is how he overturned all Dr. Barstow's plans, by coming in a large carriage instead of the cars. Strange upon what trivialities human destinies are dependent ! Now that the Doctor's well-laid scheme had been completely frustrated, he couldn't think of another plot which then and there would prevent Mrs. Titus from leaving the asylum, and in despair he feebly remonstrated :

"Mr. Titus, I think it is quite too much for her to go home in that carriage."

Mr. Titus's respect for Dr. Barstow's medical opinions had been materially lessened, and one look at the joyous, hopeful face of his wife, fairly radiant with the thought that at last she was to leave her gaol and gaoler, and be again free, gave the lie direct to the Doctor's anxiety. So, without more ado, her husband saw that she was placed comfortably in the vehicle, stepped in himself, and in a moment more they were driven off, away from Sandford Hall and its inmates.

The relatives of the family pretended not to know where

she had been. If their account be true, they had supposed her visiting in Philadelphia. They expressed pleasure at having her back again ; but inconsistently enough, soon displayed the old desire to get rid of her. Jacob Conklin was the only one who did not disguise, or attempt to disguise his real feelings.

"I am sorry thy mother is at liberty," he said to one of her daughters, a short time after her release. A very praiseworthy and brotherly feeling must have dictated the remark ; but to all those who look with horror on this man as being in, but not of the human family, let us give his own palliation of his offense. He was "divinely directed." As we all know, the Society of Friends is very dependent on heavenly guidance ; but how any one could be directed by divinity to shut up a good, true, delicate woman, subject her to every description of cruelty, with the design of keeping her a prisoner until she shuffled off either sense or life, is more than our carnal judgment can understand. But Mrs. Titus's trouble did not cease with her imprisonment ; the vindictiveness of envious relatives was not yet appeased. She had a bad cough, and needed change of air. The trip to Norfolk had been postponed indefinitely, and now she endeavored to have it again decided upon. The spies by which she was surrounded, hearing of this, went to her husband with the information, that she *wanted to leave him.* This was among the first hostile advances made after her deliverance from Barstow.

After long prayerful deliberation, she decided to bring a suit against Sandford Hall. Her daughter Emma had worried about her supposed insanity, and her cruel imprisonment, until she had gradually lost strength and health, and now, upon her mother's release, was in a settled consumption ; and while contemplating this and other sorrows resulting (directly or indirectly) from her imprisonment, Mrs. Titus decided that if there was any justice in the land, it should be meted out to those who had so foully injured her. Jacob Conklin, upon hearing of this decision, went to Mr. Titus, and told him that if such thing was attempted, *she should be put back in the asylum.* A fine threat from a man whose reputation, morality, and social position are unquestionable ! Mr. Titus said little to his wife, but was manifestly worried. Nothing daunted, she went on with her suit, attending lawyers, taking care of a sick daughter, and mixing matters generally, in a methodical way, utterly at variance with her reported insanity. The medical attendance of her daughter, Drs. Evans and Peterson, while in their professional calls upon the young girl, kept an eye to the mental condition of her nurse ; and decided that, if Mrs. Titus was insane, all the world must be a lunatic asylum. And now, while on the subject of physicians, let us record an instance of how the insanity business is conducted in these free and enlightened United States. Dr. Griscomb was called upon by some of the relatives of Mrs. Titus, interested in her remaining at Sandford Hall, and requested to present them with a certificate, declaring her to be an unsafe person to travel alone. This obliging physician immediately complied with their request, and, *without having seen the person in question,* drew up the desired certificate. Now looking at these things in a plain, unprejudiced manner, who can help shuddering at thought of the power wielded by medical practitioners ? Dr. Griscomb's behavior could hardly be classed with that of Drs. Post and Barstow. He was simply a man who, to confer a favor, would be likely to involve himself in serious difficulty ; for shortly after, happening to meet and converse with Mrs. Titus, he perceived the net into which he had been innocently drawn, retracted the certificate previously made out, and drew up another declaring her perfectly sane. No one has a right to give a medical statement of any individual's mental condition, without even

having examined that individual professionally ; and such
a proceeding, if made a State's prison offense, would save
much terrible suffering.

Mrs. Titus, after commencing the suit against Sandford
Hall, discovered that the defense was entirely sustained
by her brother, Jacob Conklin, who paid the lawyers on
the opposite side, and took upon himself the whole trouble
of the suit. So, thinking that he might just as well be engaged in conducting his own business, Mrs. Titus began
another suit against him. Then there was excitement in
earnest ! Now, notice how systematically Mr. Conklin
went to work to defeat her ends. Knowing that she
could carry on neither suit without money, and knowing
also that Mr. Titus provided her with all she used, he and
William Thomas Willetts waited on said provider with the
old story of his wife's insanity, worked over for a new
purpose. They argued that she was an unsafe person to
handle money, and he must only give her enough for the
commonest necessaries. So Mr. Titus, whose placableness
had returned after his one act of self-assertion, agreed to
their proposition—or rather *demand*. Mrs. Titus was then
taking care of her sick child in New York City, and Mr.
Titus decided that twenty dollars per week—which little
more than covered their board—would be sufficient for
both. Twenty dollars per week for the support of two
women in Gotham—one an invalid, requiring the delica-
cies which we all know cost so dearly—while thirty dollars
weekly was not considered too much to pay for the mother
alone at Sandford Hall !

But all these difficulties were powerless to daunt her.
She continued the suits. And perceiving that something
else must be tried, Dr. Griscomb—whose presence was
necessary to a hearing of the case—went to Europe.
The trial was postponed until his return. Then Jacob
Conklin experienced a new but great desire to travel, and

just before the coming back of the first wanderer, he also started for foreign shores, and the suit had to be put off further than ever. During their absence, Lydia Willetts—who appears to be a nineteenth century Catharine de Medicis—sent for Mr. Titus, and after entertaining him with the old story of his wife's insanity, closed the interview with the information that she *must be shut up again.*

Poor Mr. Titus was in a quandary !—men of his peculiar stamp generally are. The enemy were pressing forward. They carried a great many putty-blowers, which he mistook for guns, and fearful of—he scarcely knew what—anxious for peace, and dreading war, he effected a kind of compromise with the sinister-minded dame, and proceeded to the office of Drs. Evans and Peterson for the purpose of getting a certificate of his wife's insanity. These two physicians were devoid of neither conscience nor sense. They believed Mrs. Titus's reasoning powers to be perfectly sound—believed her mind to be not one particle deranged, and were certain that her brain was far superior to the many who had vainly arranged plans to get her out of the way ; so, with no undue hesitation, they refused to accede to his request. Unsuccessful in this application, and desirous of having the matter settled in one way or the other, Mr. Titus next called on Dr. Ely, of White Plains, and made a similar request. This was refused most unceremoniously, and the bewildered husband made no further attempt to assure himself of her mental unsoundness.

After a while, the two travelers—Griscomb and Conklin—returned to America, when the suits were recommenced, and hostilities went on as before their departure. The suit against Sandford Hall was first on the tapis, and was brought before a judge on the 18th of April, 1866. The course of the defense was noteworthy. They had money—Mrs. Titus had none, or about as bad. She had sufficient to pay a cheap lawyer. Well, that was enough were he an honorable man, for the veriest legal whipper-snapper that hangs round the Tombs could have won that case, and gained the damages required. She had proof in abundance of everything she asserted. Witnesses of the highest reputation were willing to testify to the truth of her complaint, and legally the defense were without a loop-hole of escape. But money is power! and the defense realizing that little fact thoroughly, endeavored, success-fully, to impress it upon others. The lawyers for the prosecution were *bribed* to lose the case. Not only the lawyers, but the judge was bribed, and his charge to the jury was no more nor less than a command. Think of a judge in this enlightened century charging a jury after this fashion: "No vindictiveness is apparent. Where no vindictiveness is proven, there can be no damages award-ed." In other words: "Bring in a verdict for the de-fense." They accepted the bribe, but it was impossible to render the service required in return. The case could not be lost, and although the counsel for Mrs. Titus did their disgraceful *worst*, scarcely made a single point, and in every way endeavored to give the defense the ad-vantage, their efforts proved unsuccessful. The jury brought in a verdict for the prosecution, but made the damages only six cents. This may seem a very contemp-tible sum, but it saved the prosecution considerable ex-pense ; for the defense were obliged, notwithstanding their dishonorable undermining, to pay the costs of the court. Their chagrin passes description! They had worked hard and burrowed deeply, but had not gained utterly. So, gaining wisdom by experience, Jacob Conklin managed his own suit in an even more villainous way. He had time to work in, and money to work with. That he ne-glected neither, the result will show. The trial was to be held some few weeks after the one against Sandford Hall.

Upon the day appointed, Mrs. Titus appeared armed with witnesses and proof of the most decided character. But they did her no good ; for the trial could not be gone on with—neither of her two lawyers appeared ! And with a triumphant expression, Jacob Conklin, the defendant, walked out of the place.

Many will think this story incredible ! Lawyers, as a class, are interested in the gaining of cases wherein they are employed, and do not like to lay themselves liable to the charge of treachery, etc. This was an exceptional case ! We admit these premises of the unbelievers ; but when they consider the circumstances, they may arrive at a different conclusion. The pecuniary position of Mrs. Titus, as explained before, did not warrant her in retaining first-class counsel ! She was obliged to procure the cheapest kind of assistance. Those who work for small sums, are generally poor. This proposition is self-evident ! Poor men need money ! Another axiom beyond dispute ! Jacob Conklin saw the pecuniary position of the lawyers his sister had engaged, and offered them much more than she could afford to pay, if they would consent to serve his ends instead of the party for whom they were retained. Lawyers who work for petty pittances have seldom any reputation worth speaking of. What one does not possess, one can not lose. They thought the matter over, concluded that his offer was the most agreeable, accepted the money, and remained away from court. A second trial was fixed upon, but to no better purpose. Neither of the legal rascals employed by the prosecution made their appearance, and finally Mrs. Titus gave up the suit.

Alone, and single handed, it was impossible to fight the terrible odds arrayed against her. This she saw, and not being a woman to waste time and strength on impossibilities, she washed her hands of the law, and gave her entire attention to her daughter, whose days upon the earth were visibly few.

Even then the family could not rest content. Her legal efforts had aroused new vindictiveness. They saw that she would be dangerous to their reputations if not put away again ; and Mrs. Titus discovering their desire to reincarcerate her in Sandford Hall, took every imaginable precaution against being again deceived. She informed the chief of the Metropolitan Police of her fears, and their cause. He listened to her story, weighed with professional acumen the different points, and ended by sending one of the staff, in citizen's clothing, to guard her home.

The twenty dollars per week allowed by Mr. Titus for the support of the mother and dying daughter, although it supplied them with indispensables, did not and could not cover the numberless little delicate desires of the invalid, who, owing to this lack of money, was often obliged to dispense with luxuries, the possession of which might have prolonged her life considerably. Knowing of this another trap was laid, into which it was thought Mrs. Titus might be inveigled. Robert Willetts, who lived in fine style some few blocks above where the two women boarded, called down upon them in his carriage, and offered to take the young consumptive to his home, where she could be surrounded by everything beautiful, and possess all she might desire.

"Oh, no !" said the child, "I can't leave mother."

"No need of that," responded Mr. Willetts eagerly. "Thy mother can go also, and the servants will relieve her from much care."

Mrs. Titus regarded this offer with suspicion ; and no wonder ! During all the time of their stay in New York, the Willetts family had offered them not the slightest courtesy ; but now, when she was hourly expecting some new stratagem of the enemy, the head of the family appears and proffers them both a home. This unexpected proposal was considered and declined, and Robert Willetts left the house foiled. Mrs. Titus having escaped this snare did not fall into another, and has succeeded in retaining her liberty, notwithstanding her enemies' persistent efforts. Now so many are aware of her unfortunate experience, that were she to disappear, but for one day, a hue and cry would be immediately raised. This the family know, and she is consequently safe.

It seems hard to attribute such deliberate villainy to so many of our first citizens ; but the facts are there, and can not be disproved. One question presents itself to our mind continually : Is Jacob Conklin not in the condition he has been so anxious to fasten upon his sister ? That upon him does not rest, as has been supposed, the whole blame of the transaction, is proven by the fact that the second attempt to abduct her was made by Lydia Willetts while he was in Europe. The conduct of the Willettses, and others, can be attributed to innate jealousies and meannesses ; but the behavior of her own brother can be accounted for on no such uncharitable hypothesis. Insanity seems the fairest explanation ! Under that head we can understand his belief in his sister's lunacy ; and if such be the case, Mrs. Titus, as one of his nearest relatives, would never recommend for his mental recuperation a stay at Sandford Hall, with its hospitable proprietor, Dr. Barstow.